To Tom Feelings and his Middle Passage,
and to a true role model, Ida Williams Thompson
—J. E. R.

ATHENEUM BOOKS FOR YOUNG READERS
An imprint of Simon & Schuster Children's Publishing Division
1230 Avenue of the Americas, New York, New York 10020
Copyright © 2019 by James Ransome
All rights reserved, including the right of reproduction in whole or in part in any form.
ATHENEUM BOOKS FOR YOUNG READERS is a registered trademark of Simon & Schuster, Inc.
Atheneum logo is a trademark of Simon & Schuster, Inc.
For information about special discounts for bulk purchases, please contact Simon & Schuster Special Sales
at 1-866-506-1949 or business@simonandschuster.com.
The Simon & Schuster Speakers Bureau can bring authors to your live event. For more information or to book an event,
contact the Simon & Schuster Speakers Bureau at 1-866-248-3049 or visit our website at www.simonspeakers.com.
Book design by Sonia Chaghatzbanian
The text for this book was set in Archer.
The illustrations for this book were rendered in acrylics.
Manufactured in China
1018 SCP
First Edition
2 4 6 8 10 9 7 5 3 1
Library of Congress Cataloging-in-Publication Data
Names: Ransome, James, author, illustrator.
Title: The bell rang / James E. Ransome.
Description: First edition. | New York : Atheneum Books for Young Readers, [2019] | "A Caitlyn Dlouhy Book." | Summary: A slave family
is distressed when they discover their son Ben has escaped to freedom.
Identifiers: LCCN 2018020589 | ISBN 9781442421134 (hardcover) | ISBN 9781481476713 (eBook)
Subjects: | CYAC: Slavery—Fiction. | Fugitive slaves—Fiction. | African Americans—Fiction. | Family life—Fiction.
Classification: LCC PZ7.R1755 Be 2019 | DDC [E]—dc23 LC record available at https://lccn.loc.gov/2018020589

The Bell Rang

The Bell Rang

JAMES E. RANSOME

A Caitlyn Dlouhy Book • Atheneum Books for Young Readers • New York London Toronto Sydney New Delhi

Monday

The bell rings,
and no sun in the sky.
Daddy gathers wood.
Mama cooks.
We eat.

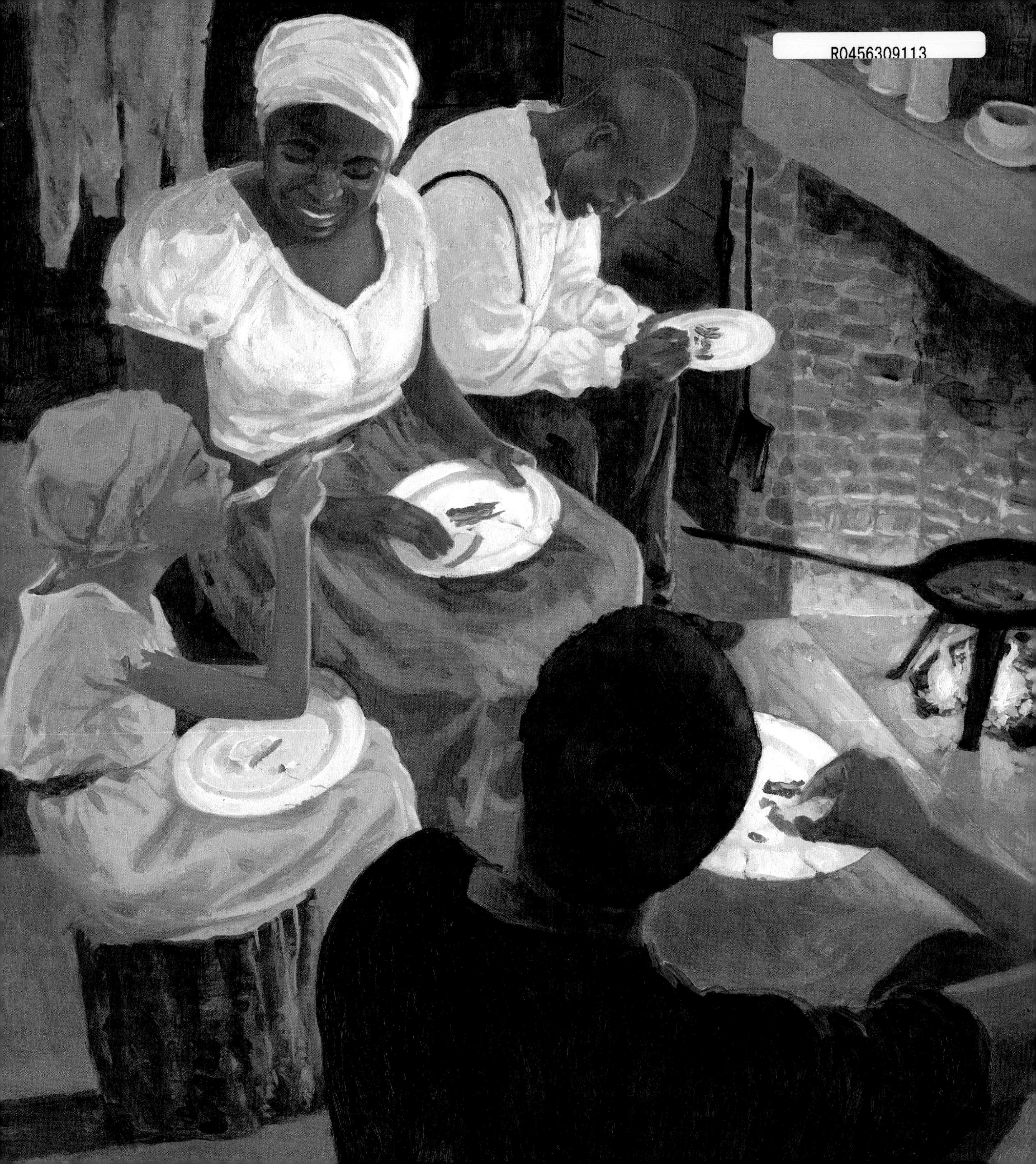

Mama kisses me.
Daddy hugs me.
My brother Ben
touches my shoulder
good-bye.

They walk to the fields
with the overseer
and Master Tucker's
other slaves.
    I go with Miss Sarah Mae
and all the young'uns.

Tuesday

The bell rings.
Daddy gathers wood.
Mama cooks.
We eat.

Mama hugs me.
Daddy's rough hands
slide down my arms.
Ben waves
good-bye.

They walk to the fields
with big hoes
for chopping.
I skip to Miss Sarah Mae's
with all the young'uns.

Wednesday

The bell rings.
Daddy gathers wood.
Mama cooks.
We eat.

Mama kisses me.
Daddy touches my neck
with rough hands.

Ben surprises me,
first with a kiss on the cheek,
then whispering
"Good-bye"
in my ear.
From behind his back
he hands me a real pretty doll.

Ben runs to catch up
with his friends Joe and Little Sam.
They walk to the field.

I run to Miss Sarah Mae's.

The doll is made
of twisted sticks
and fancy cloth
that must have come
from the master's house.
I love it
and name it Miz Ida,
after Mama.

We jump rope
together.

We play
hide-and-seek.
Miz Ida hides
with me.
We hopscotch
together.
I care for
and hug
Miz Ida all day.

Thursday

I wake to the sound
of Mama and Daddy
searching,
looking.
No sun in the sky.
Mama crying.
No Ben.
Daddy crying.
Ben ran.

We cry, we cry.

Overseer comes
to our cabin.
Then dogs come.
Overseer hits Mama,
then Daddy.
I hide.

Ben gone.
Joe and Little Sam all ran.
Mama cries
all the way to the field.
Daddy's face
looks all wrong
as he walks
with other slaves.
Many with mad looks,
some with tears.
Overseer has his gun.
I walk
to Miss Sarah Mae's.
I cry all day.

Friday

Bell rings.
Daddy gathers wood.
Mama cooks.
We're quiet.
I can't eat.

I hold Miz Ida
at Miss Sarah Mae's.
But I don't talk or play.

Saturday

Bell rings.
Daddy gathers wood.
Mama cooks.
We eat.

I kiss Mama and Daddy
good-bye.
Short work day.
They stop when the sun is high.
We think of Ben's smile.
We talk of Ben.
Ben's touch.
We miss him.
We hope he's free
like the birds.

I work with Mama
in our garden,
Daddy off fishing.

Dogs!
That's dogs barking.
Horses!
That's horses running.
"Ben!" I yell.

Slaves come from all over.
Mama puts her arms around me.
Master Tucker rides in.
Overseer rides in.
The dogs are barking
at Joe
and Little Sam.
No Ben?
They go to the tree.

Out comes the whip.

All night we cry and pray for Ben.

Sunday

No bell.
We eat.
We walk with all
of Master Tucker's slaves
to the creek.
Big Sam preach.
He preach of Moses.
He preach of being free.
We sing.
We hope.
We pray
Ben made it.

Free like the birds.
Free like Moses.
No more bells.

Monday. . .